The True Story of
Santa Claus

CHRISTINA & ERIC WALTERS

Illustrated by

ANDREW GOODERHAM

Chestnut Publishing Group

Library and Archives Canada Cataloguing in Publication

Walters, Eric, 1957-
    The true story of Santa Claus / Eric Walters, Christina
    Walters ; illustrator, Andrew Gooderham.

ISBN 1-894601-11-4

1. Santa Claus--Juvenile fiction. I. Walters, Christina
II. Gooderham, Andrew, 1971- III. Title.

PS8595.A598T78 2004   jC813'.54   C2004-905192-X

Printed and bound in Canada

Published by Chestnut Publishing Group
4005 Broadway Ave., Ste. 610
Toronto, ON M2M 3Z9 Canada
Tel: 416 224-5824 Fax: 416 486-4752
www.chestnutpublishing.com

This book is dedicated to the millions of mothers around the world who already knew how hard every Mrs. Claus works to make Christmas so special for her family.

Everybody knows that behind every great man there's a woman. But not many people know that behind every fat jolly elf there's a woman too. That's me, Mrs. Claus.

I'm the power behind the throne, or I guess more correctly, the power behind the sleigh, and it's time I stepped out and told the *true* story of Santa Claus.

Now everybody deserves a holiday. A week, two weeks or even a month seems reasonable. But my dear husband takes three hundred and sixty-four days off every year. He only works one day—actually only part of one day—Christmas Eve. I'd be the last person to say that he doesn't work hard on that one day, but facts are facts. Nobody deserves that much holiday.

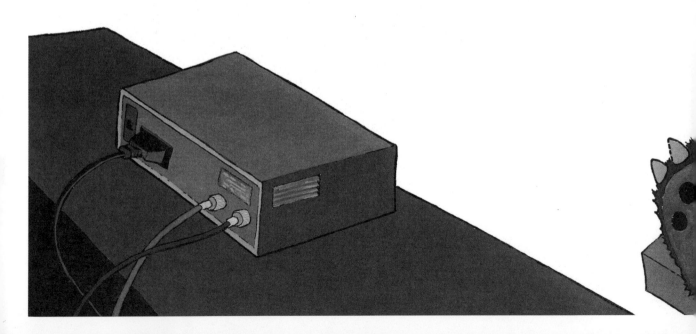

It wasn't always that way. Santa used to work almost non-stop. There's always something to be done up here at the North Pole. And I'm talking about more than just the "glamour jobs"—reading letters, making lists (and checking them twice) and, of course, making toys. There are a lot of other things that have to be done to keep Christmas up and running. Jobs like filing flight paths, mending harnesses, painting and oiling and waxing the sleigh, feeding and brushing the reindeer, and, of course, keeping house for Santa and all those elves. There was enough work to keep everybody busy. And then the trouble began.

About 50 years ago—must I remind you that elves live a very, very long time—most of Santa's helpers caught the flu and Santa was over his head in work. It looked as if there were a whole lot of good boys and girls who weren't going to be seeing any toys that Christmas.

That's when I stepped in. Being the kind person, and devoted wife, that I am, I dropped all my regular jobs and went to help Santa with his work.

And believe me, we did a fine job. Everyone said it was just about the very best Christmas that anybody could ever remember.

By the following Christmas season all the elves were healthy again and working as hard as usual. But I had gotten into the habit of helping around the Workshop as well, and I did enjoy the work, so I kept on pitching in, doing one thing or another. It was fun. At least fun at first.

Then I started to notice that more and more, there was less and less of my dear husband. He kept slipping away from the Workshop.

It all started innocently enough. We got a TV. For years it had just a few fuzzy stations. Then we got cable. Next came a big screen TV and an even bigger lazy boy lounge chair. And then Santa discovered the all sports network. Soon all he did was watch TV. Football, hockey, wrestling, fishing, the lumberjack competition, and monster truck rallies.

When I tried to convince him he needed to come back to work he would say he was already "working".

"You really need to get back to the Workshop, dear," I said.

"I'm doing R and D," he replied.

"R and D? What is R and D?" I demanded.

"Research and Development," he explained. "I have to keep on top of the new toy market!"

Ha! R and D, my foot! The only R and D he was doing in that chair was Reclining and Dining.

I think he would have starved to death if I hadn't brought his meals to him. He just sat there, his meal on the little TV table, eating and watching.

And that, of course, led to another problem. You may have noticed that over the years Santa has put on a little bit of weight. He didn't used to be so...how should I say this? Um, portly...hefty...um, stout. Oh, whom am I fooling? The man is fat.

I know there are some of you who probably think that Santa was always that way, but he wasn't. When I first met him, and you have to remember that was almost two hundred years ago, he was a major hunk. It still makes my heart go all aflutter when I think of him: short white beard, slim, trim, and muscular.

But then again, why shouldn't he be fit? If you think thirty minutes a day on a Stairmaster will make you a hard body, what do you think climbing up and down millions of chimneys would do for you? That was in the days before children used to leave a snack for him. I'd love to get a hold of the person who had the bright idea of giving him milk and cookies. What exactly is wrong with mineral water and rice cakes?

So you have to understand that it wasn't just that I was getting tired of doing all the work but that I was truly worried about my dear husband's health. I tried to talk to him, mainly during the commercials, but he wouldn't listen.

Sometimes that man can be so thick. Any time we have a disagreement he just ends it by saying, "How can you accuse me of doing anything wrong? Don't you remember, I'm a saint—Saint Nicholas."

A saint, ha! How many saints do you know who leave their clothes lying around in piles on the floor, or who put empty cartons of milk back in the fridge, or leave the toilet seat up?

So since he wouldn't listen to reason it was time to launch my plan. I came down with a terrible case of hiccumititus. It's a terrible illness. You can't stop hiccuping and your face breaks out in colourful dots—dots the same colour as the multi-pack of Crayola markers. And the only cure for this affliction is to remain in bed, drink nothing but gallons and gallons of hot chocolate, and do absolutely no work. I imagine you've never heard of hiccumititus, and there's a good reason for that. I made it up. Remember, it isn't me who claims to be a saint.

My unfortunate illness drove my husband out of his easy chair and back into the work force. Between getting me hot chocolate and being in the Workshop he was going night and day. When he did take a break, sitting in front of the TV, he'd be asleep within minutes, snoring away.

When I heard that snoring it was my cue to get out of bed, go to the Workshop, and check to make sure things were on schedule. After all, I still felt a responsibility to all the girls and boys in the world to make sure they got their presents. When I found things behind schedule I'd sneak over to Santa, still sleeping in his chair, and whisper in his ear, "You have to work harder my dear...work harder. Everybody's depending on you...depending on you." Then I'd return to my bed.

In the morning I'd be woken up by the sounds of hammering and sawing coming from the Workshop and I knew he'd heard my message.

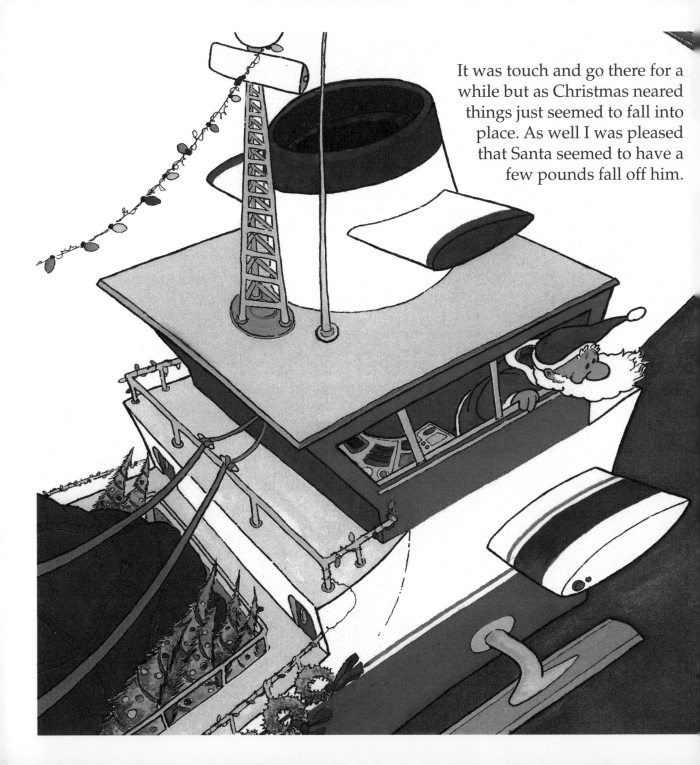

It was touch and go there for a while but as Christmas neared things just seemed to fall into place. As well I was pleased that Santa seemed to have a few pounds fall off him.

And then, miracle of miracle, as Santa set off to deliver all his presents on Christmas Eve, my case of hiccumititus was cured! The spots just seemed to vanish! It's amazing what a little soap and a washcloth can do.

Well, that was last year. This year things have been different. Between me whispering words in his ear when he's asleep, and talking to him when he's awake, he's been doing much better. Of course, it didn't hurt that every morning I get up before him and hide the TV converter. Now Santa and I run the Workshop as a team. When we work, we work together, and when we rest we sit down in our matching lazy boys and watch TV together. The strangest thing is that I'm actually starting to like watching monster truck rallies.

And while I'm still going to make sure that things never go back to the way they were before, I'm always prepared to come down with another attack of hiccumititus. I still have the markers.